A JAPANESE FOLKTALE TOBEI

retold by Mae Durham • pictures by Mitsu Yashima

Bradbury Press • Scarsdale, New York

TOBEI

At one time in the long, long ago, there lived a man, Tobei by name. He knew how to dig the *imo*.

There is this you must know about the *imo*. Delicious though it is to eat, it is most difficult to find. When it is

ripe, buried deep in the earth, its leaves above the ground
are withered. Only a sharp eye can seek the *imo* out. And it
is even more difficult to dig it up for its long, long roots
reach far down below the ground.

As it was, one day keen sighted Tobei found what could
be nothing but an *imo* not far from his home.

He set to work, and he did work: he dug, and he dug, and he dug.

He dug all of one day and the second day. His friends and neighbors came to watch. On the third day they helped Tobei. On the fourth, fifth, and sixth days, they worked even harder.

And on the seventh day there was Tobei; there were his many friends and neighbors — pulling, pulling.

But it was Tobei who, at long last, pulled with all his strength —

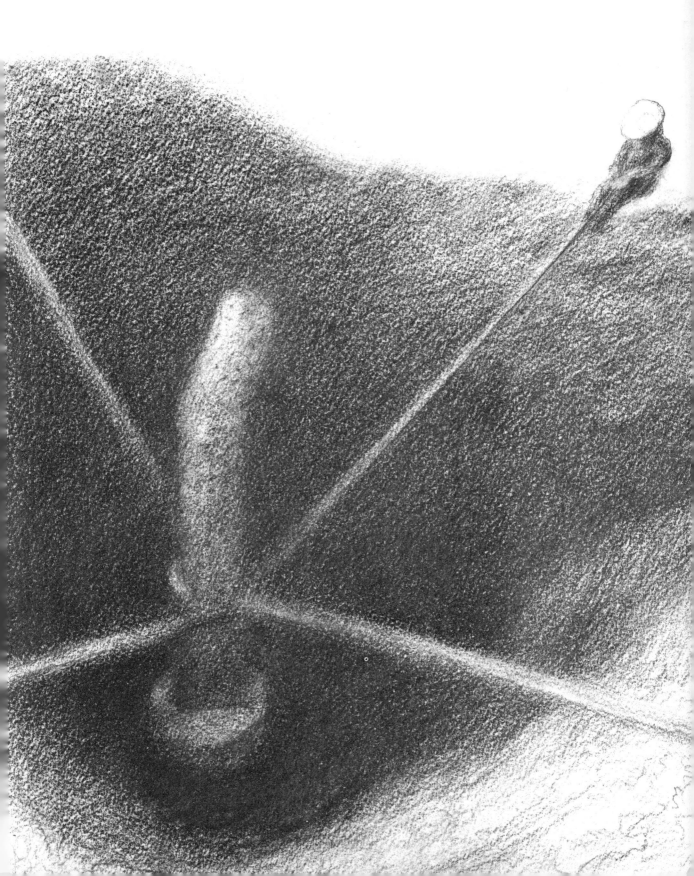

— and up came the *imo*.

Up came the *imo*, and down went Tobei into the earth.

True, it was the largest *imo* anyone had ever seen, but how to get Tobei up and out of the deep hole? Oooooi! Oooooi!

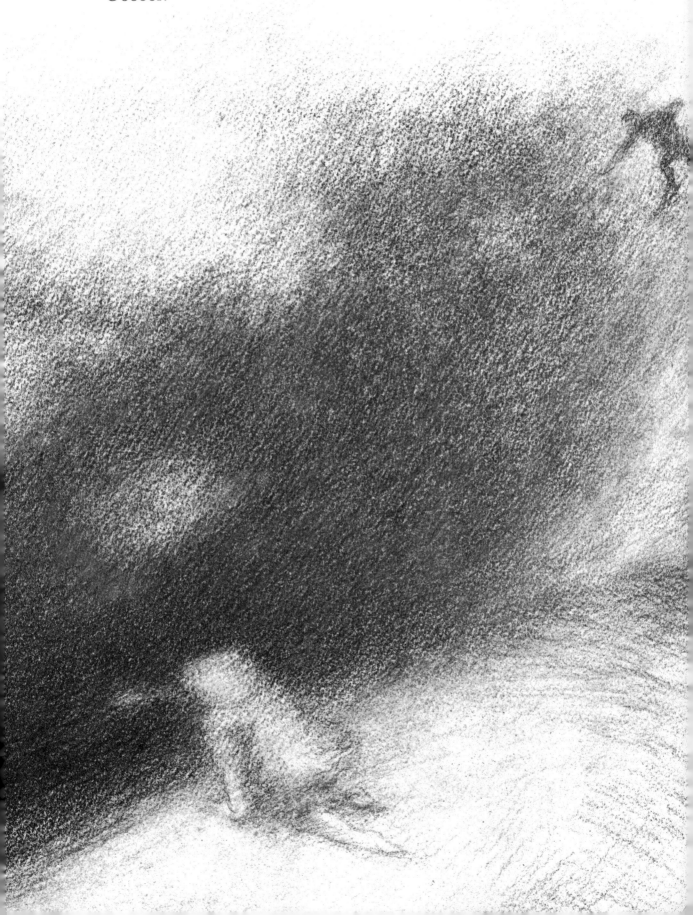

His friends and neighbors ran here, ran there, each one with a different idea.

The well basket? Its rope was not long enough.

And there was Tobei calling out, "Oooooi! Oooooi!"

The most ancient one of the village stood watching, thinking, tugging gently at his beard. Then, summoning the people together, he set forth his plan.

"First, we will make a poultice, and a large one it must be. We will mix and moisten the powder well, and spread it on paper. Just as the poultice would draw pain and soreness from the body, so might it draw Tobei up from the deep hole."

"And ancient one, what are we to do with this poultice?"

"Why, attach it to a large piece of paper or better yet, to a screen. Place the screen over the hole, and see what happens."

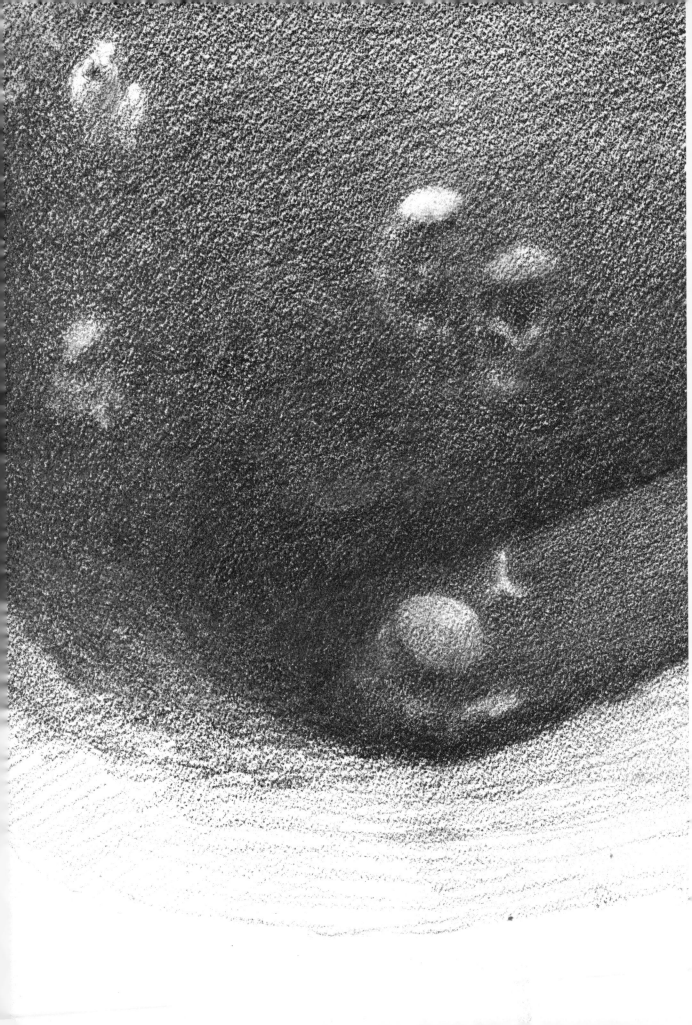

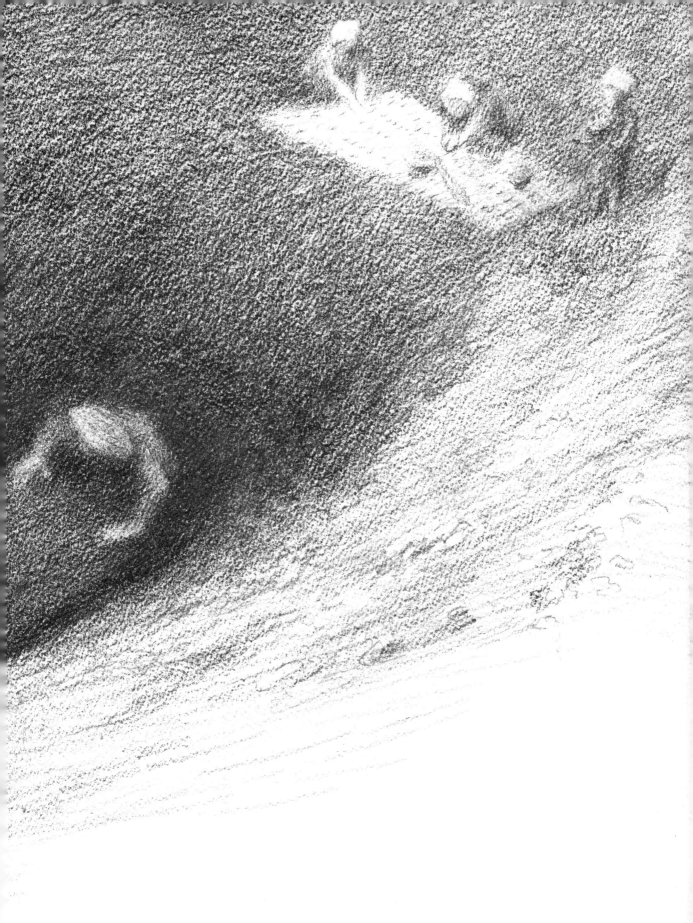

Quickly the people did as he bade them.
It happened.

The drawing power of the poultice was so great that up came Tobei quickly, more quickly than pain leaves the body. Out of the hole he came — but he could not stop. Into the air he flew, and away he went. Oooooi! Oooooi!

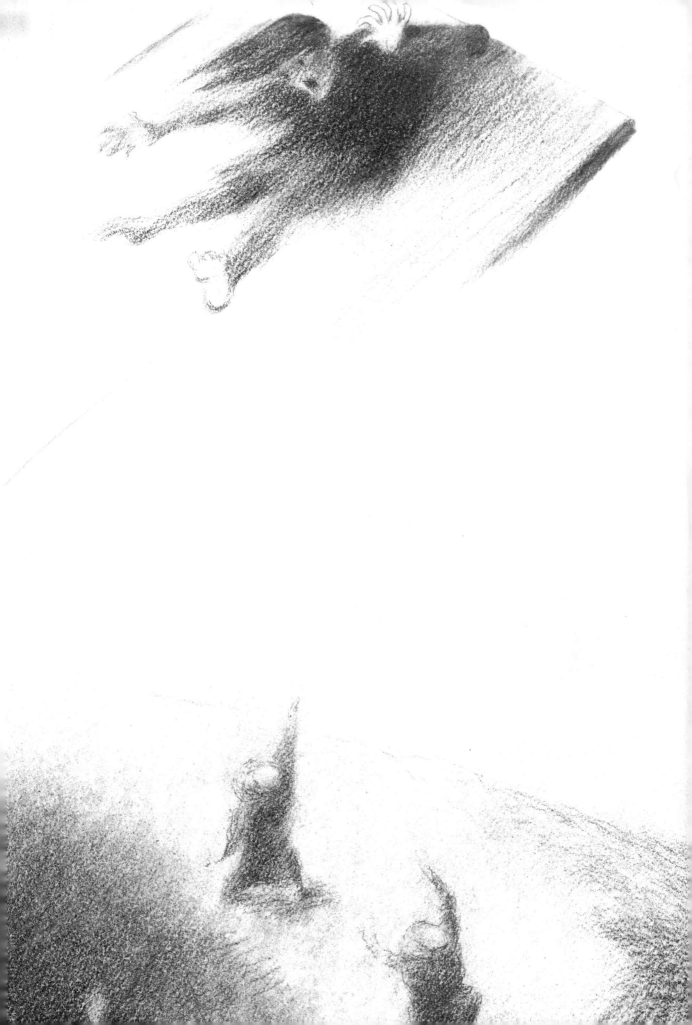

The wind carried him here and there. Oooooi! Oooooi!
On and on he flew until the wind quieted and down
came Tobei onto the roof of a temple.

He called out, "Oooooi! Oooooi!"
Hearing Tobei's voice, a priest came out of the temple
to see what he might see.

He looked up to the height of the temple, thought quickly and well. The priest ordered a large quilt to be brought, and called together four men. Each man grasped firmly a corner of the quilt.

The priest called out to Tobei, "Jump!"

Tobei jumped!

Down he came from the high roof with much vigor —

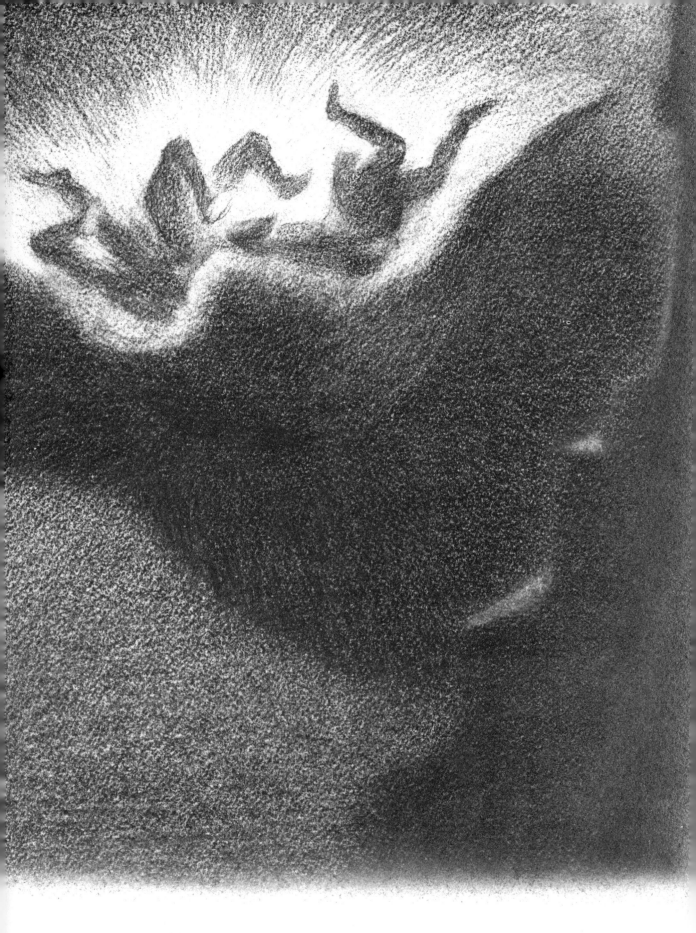

— and landed on the quilt with such force that the four men
fell forward, knocking their heads together.

Oooooi! Oooooi! Sparks flew! From the sparks came a
fire and — Oooooi! Oooooi! — the quilt caught fire!

The men caught fire! The priest, the temple caught fire!

Tobei caught fire!

ICCHIGO SAKKE DOPPEN!

And that's the end of that!